BDSM SEX COLLECTION
EXPLICIT DIRTY EROTICA SHORT STORIES

NICHOLE ROGUE

Xplicit Press
Erotica Fiction

CHAPTER 1

BECCA AND HEINKE-KERSTIN'S PONYBOY

HEINKE-KERSTIN and her best friend Becca loved to ride horses. They had the money to ride in competitions. Now they wanted to ride a human horse, a PonyBoy. Unfortunately, they didn't know any males willing to try it until Becca convinced her boyfriend Kirk; if he lost a bet, he had to do everything she wanted.

They sat around playing cards, and finally, Becca said, "Kirk if you can guess what kind of sex I really want, I'll do anything you want sexually."

"How easy is that, Kirk," Heinke-Kerstin urged him. "You two have been dating for five years now."

Kirk guessed a blowjob. Becca smiled, "Wrong," Kirk guessed an anal fuck.

"Wrong," replied Becca and giggled. "It's right in front of your face." "One left to go, "Heinke-Kerstin laughed.

"You want someone to love you." Kirk got up and danced as if at a rave party. "Absolutely wrong, sex and love are totally different."

"Why do all men think women want love? Maybe... Maybe we want sex! More sex!" "They think with their little head," Heinke-Kerstin smiled slowly, as she rubbed her thighs together under the table. "To men, love is sex!"

"How ridiculous!" groaned Becca.

The two girls had been planning this for one year now. Becca was Heinke-Kerstin's PonyGirl for that year. Becca didn't mind letting her best girlfriend forever, since fifth grade, ride her back. Becca didn't mind having a leather-covered metal bit in her mouth. "You should convince Kirk to become a PonyBoy, Becca."

Becca agreed. Now, Becca and Heinke-Kerstin celebrated by dancing together. They were gracious enough to allow Kirk to join them. The three of them danced together arm and arm. "I willingly agreed to do whatever you want. I'm willing to do my duty."

"You'll become a PonyBoy tomorrow afternoon and love it," Becca snarled and she mussed his short brown hair like he was a horse and whinnied for him.

Heinke-Kerstin laughed. "Stop that, I'm not a horse." "Not tonight, but tomorrow." Kirk was quiet.

When Kirk came over to Heinke-Kerstin's pink-outfitted basement dungeon, he found Becca there already in her cutoff jean shorts and emerald green strappy top. Kirk was told not to overdress. He wore yoga shorts and a long black leather coat down to his ankles.

Winter had set in and now there was little horse sporting activity to be had.

Heinke-Kerstin wore her black designer ankle combat

boots and her red riding cap. In her left hand, she flexed her black riding crop, shaped like a vulva at the end. Other than those clothes, she was naked.

Kirk's eyes roamed all over her naked body until Becca stepped in front of him and said, "Horses don't find women sexually attractive, PonyBoy!" Then she went and hugged her boyfriend. "You have a long way to go."

Becca removed Kirk's coat as the redheaded Heinke-Kerstin stroked his tight abs and thick pectoral muscles. "You said he ran all the time," she said as she felt his body. Next were his taut buttocks. She pinched his dusky brown nipples until they hardened.

"He lifts weights occasionally. He hides behind all those oversized clothes Hmmmmmm."

She slid a finger down his naked chest until she caught the elastic of his yoga shorts. "He's a tasty treat, but shouldn't those yoga shorts come off first?"

After Becca undressed Kirk, she said, "Kneel."

Kirk smiled. Becca and Heinke-Kerstin observed as Kirk's eyes feasted on the two women's gorgeous bodies.

.   .   .

"First I'll let Becca demonstrate. Undress Becca." Becca undressed completely.

"Kneel, PonyGirl!"

Becca went on all fours. Heinke-Kerstin held up a hand-length black leather rod, attached to leather straps. "This is a bit. You've seen in horses. All horses wear a bit so their owner and rider can more easily control them."

Becca willingly opened her mouth, but said before accepting the bit, "I've been Heinke-Kerstin's PonyGirl for a year now. I know everything you're going to go through, Kirk."

Kirk laughed up a storm. He flexed his biceps and posed like Mr. Universe. "I can hold up a little one-hundred and eighteen-pound beauty."

Becca gave an expression *he has it down all ready*. She and Heinke-Kerstin laughed together. Heinke-Kerstin put the bit into Becca's mouth. It's not as easy as all that, Kirk." She turned, "I'll be right back."

Kirk loved looking at Becca's blonde bushy twat. He loved how it juiced up nicely. He started to bend down and lick her pussy, but Becca whinnied loudly and galloped away on her hands and knees too fast.

Heinke-Kerstin came back quickly holding an American-style saddle with the stud in the middle. Perfect for a girl riding side-saddle or for a girl to masturbate her clit against. "What are you doing to my horse, Kirk!"

"I—I wasn't—" He stopped and looked at Becca and then Heinke-Kerstin. Kirk's guilt shows all over his face. He shrugged.

"Now down on all fours, Kirk." Heinke-Kerstin turned to Becca and said, You can get up now."

Becca's facial expression changed to glee. "See how serious I was during our pony play?" Kirk whinnied and shook his head diagonal-sideways like horses do.

Heinke-Kerstin said, "He's good."

"We will see if he fulfills the bet." Becca pointed to the small clock on the wall. "Of course, horses can't tell time, that's why the clock is so small. But you have one hour of PonyBoy play to complete."

Kirk backed up a couple crawls and came forward so that the two women could pat his head. He gave a soft whinnied again.

"Aw," the girls said.

Becca saddled Kirk up. She strapped the saddle behind his thighs and under his massive chest. She made sure the saddle wouldn't roll over under him. "Your horse is ready, Mistress Heinke- Kerstin."

Mistress Heinke-Kerstin spread her legs wide and straddled Kirk's strong back. When she sat down, she did so slowly, giving him a chance to hold her up. Becca saw Kirk trying to figure out how she held up her Mistress because her weight seemed quite heavy now.

"We did not add any weight to the saddle, Kirk," Becca said.

Kirk nodded his head two times like a horse, wanting to eat some grass.

Mistress Heinke-Kerstin put her foot in the stirrups, reached behind with the crop, and slapped his ass. Kirk jerked and started moving forward.

Becca's pussy oiled up and overflowed in no time. She

followed behind them as Mistress Heinke-Kerstin taught Kirk some basic moves, forward, back, circle left and right. She brought him to a halt and leaned down over his back and neck and whispered in Kirk's ear, "Becca loves to have her own PonyBoy."

Kirk shook his head sideways, No. Heinke-Kerstin raised up and started riding him faster in long looping curves back and forth over the soft carpet. She brought him to a halt and let Becca masturbate Kirk until his dick meat jutted out hard. His prick pointed the way forward and even a long line of his pre-cum dripped onto the carpet. Becca bit her lip.

Mistress Heinke-Kerstin repeated the maneuvers and brought Kirk to a stop. She leaned over on his back and whispered into his ear again. She knew Kirk was tired.

"Becca said the hour is only half up. He's going to fail." "I've whispered a way out of the bet. To satisfy it."

"Kirk please answer. Show me you can ride longer than me. I'm just a girl," Becca whinnied loud.

Kirk's green eyes look bewildered at first. Then they calmed down and Kirk nodded, Yes. "You might as well start now, "Heinke-Kerstin ordered.

Becca reached from behind his legs and cupped his huge balls. Kirk's dick hardened to steel and a thick line of sperm spurted from his jutting prick all over the carpet. He arched his back and another blob of his man spunk hit the carpet.

"He's coming, Mistress Heinke-Kerstin. I'd say that's an

unconscious, yes!" Mistress Heinke-Kerstin dismounted. Her girleygoo flowed all over the saddle seat.

"Oh look at that thick white goo he shot out. He's excited to ride me," Becca said carefully mounting Kirk. Becca took the vulva riding crop after putting her foot in the stirrups. She slapped his softening dick lightly. She slapped his thigh and said, "Go PonyBoy! Go!

Weeeeeee!"

Kirk Whinnied really loud and rode fast in a clockwise circle, as Becca put him through his paces.

--THE END--

CHAPTER 2

BIG O TRAINING FOR FINNISH ERTTA

ERTTA SAT on a small three-legged footstool of finely carved wood. The round seat of the multi-colored cushion caressed her tush. But Ertta was forced to sit legs wide, spread-legged on the footstool. Her fishnet silk body stocking revealed her beautiful nakedness. Her white skin glowed under the black fishnet's tiny diamonds. By degrees, Ertta experienced her sexual wants and needs. Inside her pussy slot two Ben-Wa balls rose and fell, up and down, stimulating her heated core to great delight. Mistress Hatachi put the balls in herself. She measured Ertta's cunt path. These heavy black balls made concentrating on the clock harder. When the Ben-Wa balls fell down they stimulated the sensitive lips of Ertta's dripping cunt. When she raised them up to her cervix, her clit extended further from her sweaty folds. The huge clock in front of Ertta matched her mood. It ticked slowly. The minute hand was running like the hour hand. The hour hand running like a day-hand on a chronological clock.

. . .

Behind Ertta's back, her tied hands were wrapped in her own soiled golden silk panties that kept her from moving and touching herself. Ertta knew something about masturbating, but Mistress Hatachi stopped all that. "That's why you can't cum. You fear really touching yourself. You fear you'll become insatiable. You want someone else to do it. So you can blame them for your own erotic feelings. I'll do it for you, Ertta. I'll touch you inside and outside in ways you'll never guess."

Ertta realized the Japanese woman understood more about a woman's sexual desires. Ertta breathed in and out, faster and deeper as the ripples of orgasm flowed through her entire body. The fine fishnet covering's small openings resembled diamond shapes. In her black fashionable ankle boots, Ertta found relaxing into an orgasm very difficult. How can one come with shoes on? Yet every hindrance to her orgasm brought her closer to her ultimate goal, a Big Orgasm. She'd been searching for the mighty orgasm since her teens. She went to a psychologist; she relied on men. All of the men told her fast sex was guaranteed to make her see stars. She did not see stars. Only small pitiful feelings of warmth rolled over her body. Feelings that lead to further frustration.

Ertta's inner thighs already soaked the fishnet body stocking. She had been sitting only for ten minutes. Twenty minutes remained, and then she could get up and walkabout. Only Mistress Hatachi owned the right to whip her with her heart-shaped riding crop as she walked. Ertta loved all the attention. Her heavy breasts swayed back and forth in quiet desperation. Her tight nipples responded to the restraining material by trying to squeeze through the fish-net's diamond patterns. Her nipples pressed against the silky material, more and more. Ertta's eyes shot wide open as her right nipple slipped through and sent pleasure heat flowing down her thighs and up to her throat. She blushed.

"One nipple pushed through," Mistress Hatachi came around front and pinched the annoying piece of flesh.

Ertta sighed deeply. She moaned deeply only every sound went into the black ballgag stuffed into her mouth. Or they came out as murmurs: "MMMMMM-mmmm."

"Talking stops a woman from climaxing. No woman should talk during sex unless it is to say dirty words, or to tell her lover to 'Fuck me harder! Do me faster! Fuck it! Take my cunt space up with your huge bloated cock meat!'"

Mistress Hatachi had been training Ertta for almost two months now. They had made progress. Only the Big O still escaped Finnish Ertta. However, each day the distractions stopping Ertta from climaxing slowly but surely lowered. Her Big O became more accessible each Friday session they both enjoyed together.

Ertta loved her body but didn't understand it.

Mistress Hatachi's understanding of sex flowed from

her understanding of Shintoism and Ki. Those ancient arts of subtle power. "Ertta, your skin is the largest organ on your body. Not your clit, not your brain, not your asshole or even your labia lips or cunt." Mistress Hatachi began to swish her heart-shaped riding crop around in the air. Each time Ertta jumped as her skin grew more aware, more sensitive to wind and motion.

Mistress Hatachi wore an Amazon-like black leather blouse. Beneath this, she wore a leather skirt with tiny ripples. Each ripple had a way of glancing off the living room light in Mistress Hatachi's dungeon. Light played a big part in the women's erotic games. But touch was by far the greatest sexual stimulate they shared.

Ertta's cunt convulsed hard. Her legs quivered. Her huge pussy quake neared. Her black mascara started to run from the sweat of holding all that sexual tension. Mistress Hatachi believed women needed to cum when their makeup ran down their faces. She even spritzed Ertta's face every ten minutes.

"Time for another spritz, Ertta."

Ertta shook her head. Inside she believed looking like a raccoon was not erotic. No man wanted to fuck a raccoon bride. The fine mist blasted from the sterilized water bottle. "Spriiittttzzzzzzzz. Spritttzzzz!"

Ertta's face softened. Her nude blush began to run. The highlights on the bridge of her nose, her most attractive feature, dulled. Ertta saw herself after every Friday session ended. She looked terrible. Luckily, Mistress Hatachi allowed her to use her vanity to clean up before she went home and slinked in her single bed in her small apartment all alone on the other side of town.

Ertta's shoulders slumped and her legs begged to come together. She wanted to rub them together. She needed to touch her inner thighs. Stroke her plump buttocks. Stab her long tapered fingers into her cooze box, dripping her fuck oils on the ornate footstool.

Mistress Hatachi slapped Ertta on the ass. Another slap on her ass cheek made Ertta jump. There would be heart-shaped marks on her ass, inner thighs, and breasts when this session ended.

But Ertta heaved. She swallowed on the ball gag as her orgasms rushed forward like a rocket going to the Moon.

Mistress Hatachi slapped her left tit twice. Turning like she would walk behind Ertta's back, Mistress returned counter-clockwise and slapped hard in that sacred place. Ertta's throbbing clit.

"Mmmmmm-hmmm! UUmmm-MMMMM!" Ertta's eyes shot open and closed tightly as she came! Mistress Hatachi hurriedly put a jade bowl under her pussy as the pussy squirt flowed out of her apex, over the footstool. She brought the jade bowl up and held it to Ertta's flaring pretty white nostrils. "You came. Here is the proof."

Ertta sniffed. Internally, her body continued to rock from powerful orgasmic waves. She wanted to hug Mistress Hatachi. Mistress Hatachi stepped back. Ertta slumped down on the footstool.

She knew the pleasures all the women raved about. Alone she accepted her lust. She would never despise or fear sex again. Sure, she now felt insatiable, like a horny wench, but that was a small price to pay for sexual satisfaction.

--THE END--

CHAPTER 3

BOUND UNTIL SHE CUMS

NAKED SPANISH GIRL Salvatierra Jimenez found every extremity bound in leather straps. The only part of her left unbound was her small pearly clit peeking out, as she wondered how this came to happen. Salvatierra's lower arms were strapped down on two different sides of the gymnastic-like pommel black horse apparatus. Her calves were strapped down in the same meticulous manner. Two thin black leather straps pressed her breasts to the leather seat. She wore a large golden chain; it was linked by a longer, thinner golden chain to the horse. The long thin shoulder-purse length chain gave Salvatierra just enough room to rise up and scream; just enough room to rise up and moan out her orgasms. The way her bare-naked ass spread, exposed as it was around the six-inch width leather horse-padded contraction, left her vulnerable to any type of ass or pussy insertion Mistress Luella might invent.

Luella Santiago came from Brazil. Her bondage practice needed to expand back to the old country. She always wore black fingernail polish to show strength. Her small thin hands supported her as a hand model for soaps and hair shampoos in her younger years. Luella's C cup round cantaloupe breasts often found their way loose. So thirty-five-year-old Luella started wearing open tops. Right now, she wore a black leather catsuit, her top fully exposed. Her long wavy blonde hair belied the strength with which she whipped her subjects. Her long natural lashes and big beautiful black eyes made her an unforgettable Mistress for men and women alike. Several women worked for her over the years. Salvatierra heard about Luella from her girlfriend who went abroad to Brazil for college.

When Salvatierra came to Luella for the first time, she wore a criss-cross large diamond-shaped black straps of leather under a long leather coat. Naturally, two big diamonds allowed her endowed breasts to fit through. This made her distended tits irresistibly touchable. Luella knew right away because the half-inch black straps ran over Salvatierra's clit, up her crotch, the girl was secretly trying to masturbate.

"I've just the apparatus to satisfy your lust. I will see you keep that cash. Salvati."

Strapped down like that, Salvati, as Luella took to calling her every two days, forgot about easing her own fingers down into the hot V of her crotch. She forgot all about touching that hot thin line of her cookie-shaped cunt. Her inner labia lips rolled under, not by surgery, but by nature. Each time she walked her inner labia massaged her outer labia, driving the girl crazy for lust and penetration. Penetration that must not happen, by finger, dildo, vibrator, or penis. Especially not the penis.

The beautiful Spanish girl's Mom died when Salvati turned 5 years old. Her Dad always blamed the situation on sex. Her Mom went out to buy a vibrator and died in a car crash. Salvati's Dad went into a protective rage and made fourteen-year-old Salvati, coming into her feminine bloom, sign the agreement.

Salvati went on to school like any other Spanish girl growing up in Catalonia. She heard all about the old days of Catalonia's freedom and how beautiful it was. But for Salvati, the only thing making a difference in her life was sex. She needed it more and more. She watched her girlfriends giving blowjobs, jerking boys off, and telling wild stories about sex in cars and parks.

Salvati desperately wanted to relieve her frustration, even though she often wondered during high school, how could her Dad tell if she'd masturbated?

Now that she was eighteen, only one more year remained to be chaste. If only her growing breasts didn't tease her at night. Her sensitive nipples teased her at "that time of the month." They rolled and swelled. Each breast called out for a man's touch. That's when her girlfriend from Brazil called.

"Salvati, I know how you can orgasm and not have sex!"
"Do tell me," Salvati pleaded.

"Luella Santiago runs a popular bondage and discipline club here. She is returning to Catalonia!"

"She's coming here?" Salvati sat up in her lacy white bra and panties. Her dark Spanish skin was tan making the gauzy garments look stark white and beautiful.

Her girlfriend told her more about Ms. Santiago. Her preferences and kinks. So much so, Salvati wondered if her girlfriend went under a whip session with Ms. Santiago. Her girlfriend giggled but never revealed anything.

"I just know she'll satisfy you, Salvati."

Salvati went to the castle location and knocked on the door. A man answered it. Salvati came in her cotton, bunny-covered panties under her long black skirt and white button blouse. She leaned into his arms. "I feel faint."

The man caught her and brought her inside the parlor. He used a fashion magazine to fan her. He stopped and reached for her white blouse and started to unbutton it

Luella's short stub heals clicked through on the tile floor. "Stop! What are you doing?! "I was going to open her blouse and fan her."

"She doesn't need a man. Men are the problem. Go. Fetch us some wood for the fireplace." When Salvati came to, she found herself nude and bound.

Luella heard all about her strange financial agreement. There was no time to waste. "Salvati, you need to come right away. You need to experience that magnificent orgasm to relieve your stress."

Salvati heard things, "Some called it the Big O." The coolness of the chains massaged her neck.

"Orgasms will come soon, Salvati. My apparatus is designed to bring it on without touching you."

"Thank you," was all Salvati said.

Luella waited and talked to Salvati. Luella related her adventures as a hand model. How all the young men wanted to fuck her. With each story, Salvati's pussy dripped. Her clit stretched out.

Her inner labia fluttered. Her orgasm was growing and growing. The waves moved higher and higher up her young nineteen-year-old flesh.

"You're ready, Salvati." "Ready for what?"

"Ready for Everardo Herrera to fuck you."

Salvati struggled against her restraints. "You promised to protect me!" "I am. No one will know."

"Come Everardo." "Who is Everardo?"

"The handsome man you met at the door. My twenty-two-year-old son."

Salvati's eyes rolled into the back of her head. Her body shook. Her clit drummed. Her womb jumped. Her nipples pushed her up off the leather horse as she heard his steps near. The sense of exploding captured her imagination.

. . .

Salvati's pussy suddenly squirted her heated sexual essences all over the leather horse. The wetness rolled under her legs and soaked her belly. But supreme sexual satisfaction overwhelmed all sensations.

"I came! I came!"

"That you did," said Luella smiling. "And no one has touched you."

I've kept my Dad's wishes. I believe I'll be okay now. Until my birthday on May 30."

"You'll do just fine," Mistress Luella said, unlocking the leather restraints. "And Everardo will be waiting if you want more sex on your nineteenth birthday. Just give me a call."

"I will, Luella."

--THE END--

CHAPTER 4

CEO'S NEW PROJECT

HIS CARNAL DESIRES

WHEN SARAH GOT out of bed, she was certain of one thing; today was the day that would change her life. One night of total submission that would reward her with a quarter of a million dollars. When her CEO, Mr. Sanders, brought up the idea, Sarah had thought it was totally preposterous. She now saw it as a life-changing opportunity.

She had been out until late that morning and had barely gotten a few hours of sleep. Mr. Sanders would send his driver to pick her up at exactly six this evening. Had she got enough rest? Not really, but at this moment she was desperate and would do just about anything for some extra cash. Which in her case was much more than that; Mr. Sanders was offering her a large lump sum, $250,000 to be exact.

The details of what would happen tonight were kept confidential; all she knew is that she'd have to sign a contract giving him total control of her body. She also knew that it involved some restraining. Surprisingly she was more anxious than fearful. She had heard about BDSM and had been a little curious about it for a while now.

After making herself something light to eat she took a relaxing bubble bath and sipped on a little red wine. Tonight would be a long exhausting night she presumed, and so Sarah took a few extra minutes to do some relaxing.

Soon it was time to go. The sound of the knocking on the door had her heart racing. A stout man, who introduced himself as Mr. Sander's chauffeur, picked her up and drove her to the most beautiful, extravagant mansion she'd ever been to in her entire life.

Mr. Sanders met her at the door of his mansion dressed in a black tux and invited her inside. Her heart thudded as she walked in behind him. As he led her up the winding steps in his foyer, she couldn't help but notice the dark, mysterious, luxurious feel of his house.

He led her to the last lonely room in a dark hallway upstairs. As he flicked the lights on, he locked the door behind her. To her amazement, the room was filled with sex toys and sex equipment. Before he proceeded with anything he handed Sarah a contract. He explained the details to her and asked her to sign and date the last page of the six-page document.

His fingers shook as she signed away her freedom for the night.

"Great!" he said, as his eyes lit up as he helped her onto a small platform in the center of the room. Using a rolling cart, he brought some restraining equipment closer.

"Everything's gonna be okay, just relax."

He strapped her completely naked onto the bench with her body arched backward.

He used a mouth gag to muffle her cries. Without warning, he reached into the cart a pulled out a whip. The feel of the whip against her pussy sent tiny spasms shooting through her entire body. It was weird; it felt like a sweet painful pleasure.

Soon he left her side but returned shortly with a vibrating wand, which he massaged against her clitoris. Jolts of energy shot through Sarah's body as she bucked her pussy against the device. She cried out in delirium but her cries were muffled by the mouth gag, obstructing any noise coming from her.

"So fucking beautiful," he grunted, as he carefully scrutinized every inch of her pussy. He was like a lion eyeing its prey, licking his lips as he went along. But her adventure with Mr. Sanders was just beginning. He had so much more planned for her. He reached over to his table of sex toys and retrieved a pair of nipple clamps. Her eyes shot open as he fastened the clippers onto her hardened nipples. The pain from the nipple clamps was masked by the sensation of a small butterfly-shaped device that he placed directly over her clitoris.

The humming sound of the device over her clitoris let her know exactly what type of device it was, a clit stimulator. Her eyes almost rolled in the back of her head, as sensation gripped her entire body.

"I want to hear you moan and beg for more," his tone was arrogant as he swiftly walked over to her head, and removed the mouth gag. As soon as he removed the restriction from her mouth, Sarah let out a loud cry of relief. She'd wanted to cry out for more, but couldn't, now that she was free from her mouth gag, she intended on fully expressing herself vocally. After all, this was the extent of what she could do, considering the fact that the rest of her body was bonded with rope and chain onto the bench-like equipment.

A loud shriek escaped her lips as he penetrated her

moist folds with a huge stainless steel dildo. The coldness of the dildo sent a chill through her pussy.

"Oh God, yes!" she cried out in ecstasy, as he began working the dildo in and out of her tight wet pussy. Wave after wave of pleasure seem to crash down between her legs, as her juices flowed freely.

Mr. Sanders was happy that her body was very receptive to his little torture. He could tell that she wanted to feel the real deal - his thick raw meat thrusting inside her pussy relentlessly. But he decided to hold off a little. After all, this was his little fantasy, and she was just his willing participant. And so he continued fucking her with the dildo, bringing her to the brink of her orgasm. Just when he noticed that she was about to reach her climax he pulled away.

"No! No! No!" she cried out breathlessly. Her eyes were filled with desire.

This was exactly what he wanted. Sarah Patton, fully naked, begging him to penetrate her pussy with his massive cock.

With a huge smile on his face, he whipped out his cock and stroked it a few times. He could tell that from the surprised look on her face, she hadn't expected him to be so well-endowed.

He positioned himself between her spread legs and brought his cock to the slit of her pussy. Slowly he stroked her tender flesh, teasing her.

"Please, Mr. Sanders...Now," she begged as her wet hungry pussy lay before him, inviting him to dive in.

Without further hesitation, he penetrated her core with a quick hard thrust. He pulled out quickly and served her with another hard thrust. Gradually he increased the momentum of his thrusts, slamming his cock into her wet pussy without mercy. Over and over, his shaft penetrated her temple of delight, until he could no longer control himself. With a loud moan, the two of them summated their climax.

He pulled out of her with his semi-erect cock, and slowly began releasing her from her restraints, but little did she know this was just the beginning of a long, wild erotic adventure.

CHAPTER 5

OF LOVE AND LUST

THE SOUNDS she makes as I lay on top of her are what make me want her even more. I could say I always wanted her, and it would be true. But those sounds... those sounds and the thought that they are only for me, such things sweep me along to an altogether different realm. A dream world where time stands still and the echo of her voice fashions landscapes filled with pleasure and secret desire. Her gentle purring, her soft moaning, her pleading for me not to stop, they all mix, dance in blissful unity. The memories of those sounds make me miss all the more when she's not around.

But now, right now, as I look upon her and see her eyes looking back as I caress her face and she presses it against my hand as I feel myself inside her and realize I have never been this happy, is when her sounds make me almost melt. And I do. I fade into her. We become one motion, no end of one, no start of the other. My thrusts are gentle and caring; she moves with them and meets them. My hands find their place upon her body, move only slightly, only to gently squeeze or caress. Our kisses are not mere kisses, but rather an exchange of breaths – my essence into hers and hers into mine, a circle of energy. Her touch is so tender I know I should barely feel her hands upon me, yet each touch is electric, mesmerizing like her eyes. I slip away one last time as her breathing grows deeper and her heartbeat quickens, replacing the sounds she makes with a steady drumbeat. And as I feel her all over me, watch her cum, feel her legs shake, I realize I had never seen anything more beautiful. But like the change of seasons, imperceptible and slow, her mood had slowly been changing. She stands up and gives me that look. I know that look. I have seen it before. I want that look again. I have wanted it, and when she walks away, the sound of her footfall passing, I realize what comes next.

She comes back with a large black strap-on tied over her pussy. It sways from one side to the next. I heard her sounds, now she wants to hear mine. I don't mind. I never do. She likes to play the boss and I like to indulge her. With a movement of her long finger, she indicated she wants me on my stomach. I want to see her do that pose of hers as she gets on one knee, the other leg as though standing, knee bent. I always wanted to see it, so I installed a mirror by the side of our bed. She spits on me like I am nothing, smudges her wet saliva over my ass, and spits again. She does this for a while, the hunger growing in her eyes. She wants to ram that thing into me; I can see it in her face. I spread my butt cheeks for her and she doesn't wait. With one, slow and rather careful movement, she hears me moan as I watch the thing go into me. It glistens as she begins to fuck me with it.

There's something incredibly hot about watching a woman fuck you in the ass. One side of your brain cannot truly comprehend what is happening and holds your ass tight, while the other enjoys the helplessness and the letting go. Her tits sway and bounce as she rides herself on me. She grabs her long, black hair and with a few swift motions, removes the rubber band from her wrist and ties her hair into a knot. She uses her knees to stretch my legs and hits me over the ass. I can see she enjoys the sound of it, the sight of it. She reaches low, grabs my dick and, while slowly fucking me and licking my back, begins to jerk me off.

"Turn around," she says.

She isn't asking me, she's telling me. She gets on her knees and spreads my legs as I turn on my back. This time she doesn't go slowly. She puts her whole weight behind it, my cock in her hand, as she thrusts the entire length and girth of the massive strap-on into me. Her movements quicken her jerking get more vicious. She twists her hands around my cock, spits on it, licks her palm, then continues, harder. When she sees I am on the edge, she stops.

"Not yet," she says.

I watch as she removes the strap-on, going in again, fully out, and in again. The thing drips with her spit as she spits on it every time she does this. I know what comes next. She removes the dildo, jams her fingers in my mouth, licks them, spits on them, and then slowly jams her whole fist into my ass. She lies down on her stomach and starts to fill her mouth with my rigid cock as she fists me. Her tongue dances over my cock, her lips suck on it, her eyes distant and lost in the thrill of it. She knows me so well, knows exactly when I have had enough.

"You will come for me," she says. And I do. Oh god how I do. I fill up her mouth with it; see it dripping down her chin, over her breasts, all the way to her clit. She removes the strap-on with a dexterous hand and rubs my sperm all over herself. She gets on her knees, her pussy in front of my face.

"Lick it clean."

She doesn't have to tell me twice. We both do it. I lick her pussy until she starts to moan, and she cleans her face with her fingers and licks them clean. Those sounds again. Those damn sounds of hers. She gives me the longest kiss, our breath meeting once again then looks into my eyes, smiles, and says,

"Now do me."

ABOUT THE AUTHOR

Nichole Rogue

    Nichole Rogue is an emerging erotica author of many erotica kinks and sub-genres. Be sure to check out other books and leave a review if this story got you hot!

    Visit my blog at Nichole Rogue Blog

    Join my newsletter for exclusive Nichole Rogue Newsletter

Sign up for Free Stories from Xplicit Press Authors

    Xplicit Press Author Updates

    Like Xplicit Press on Facebook

    Follow Xplicit Press on Twitter

Readers: I want to expand a few of the stories to see where the characters can be explored further. If there are any of the stories that you would like to read more about again, I'd love to hear from you!

Keep In Touch
Nichole Rogue
info@nicholerogue.com